Finsterhall of
San Pasqual

By
JOHN SINOR

Library of Congress Catalogue No. 76-20961
ISBN 0-89325-002-3

Published in the United States by Joyce Press, Inc., 4974 Cass St., San Diego,
Calif. 92109.
First Printing.

Books by John Sinor

Eleven Albatrosses in My Bluebird Tree
Finsterhall of San Pasqual

The story of Finsterhall is lovingly dedicated
eleven times, to each of our children, and just
once more, to Ted Bardacke.

I

Strangers in the Valley

Finsterhall found the track just before dusk. At least, it seemed to be a track. But, a track of what?

Maybe his eyes were playing tricks on him. He was still half asleep, having just come out of his burrow after spending the warm, daylight hours in his cool, dark bedroom under the ground.

"Hey, Joe," he yelled to his cousin, who also was waking up a few yards away. "Could you come over here for a minute and look at something?"

Joe yawned, then hopped over to the shade of the sagebrush where Finsterhall was standing.

"What is it?"

"I don't know," said Finsterhall. "Take a look at that. What does it look like to you?"

Joe examined the deep impression in the

5

Joe examined the deep impression in the earth. Then he said, "It looks like some kind of wide hole in the ground."

"Yeah?" said Finsterhall. "Well, if you'll take a closer look, you'll see that hole in the ground has toes."

earth. Then he said, "It looks like some kind of wide hole in the ground."

"Yeah?" said Finsterhall. "Well, if you'll take a closer look, you'll see that hole in the ground has toes. I think it's a track."

Joe examined it more carefully. Sure enough, it did seem to have the print of toes of a sort. Stubby ones, to be sure, but toes all the same.

He looked up at Finsterhall and twitched his nose.

"How could it be a track? It's too big to be a track. Why, that thing must be a foot across."

"Yep," said Finsterhall. "At least a foot." And his nose twitched a few times, too. "If it IS a track, and the track itself is a foot long, how big do you suppose the rest of it might be?"

"Oh, well," said Joe, "you know how tracks can fool you. Now, you and I probably leave tracks as big as any of the other characters in this valley. But neither of us weighs much more than two pounds. It's just that rabbits have big feet; at least, big back feet. On the other hand, that dumb bobcat, Pedro, weighs almost ten times what we do, and he leaves little tracks. Then there's that family of foxes on the south slope. Even smaller tracks than Pedro. And what about those horses that came through here that time? Even they didn't leave tracks THAT big. No, Finst, I just don't see how that could ..."

"Joe," Finsterhall interrupted, "have you ever heard of an animal called an elephant?"

Joe stared at his cousin for a few seconds. Then he blinked his eyes and twitched his nose. Finally he spoke.

"Finst," he said, "I think the sun was still a little too high when you came out today. This is Southern California, not Africa or India. Just a nice little country valley in Southern California. Do you feel feverish at all?"

"Nope," said Finsterhall. "I just feel that there's an elephant around here — somewhere."

Now, the idea of an elephant in San Pasqual Valley was just as silly as Joe had thought. Oh, there were plenty of other wild animals and birds, and hundreds of forms of plant life. But this was chaparral, or dwarf forest, country. No place for something as big as an elephant.

Finsterhall and Joe were in the majority among the animal types — the jackrabbits. Each had dozens of brothers and sisters, hundreds of cousins, and countless distant relatives in the valley.

Then there was Pedro, the bobcat, who liked to think of himself as sort of a miniature lion — king of the dwarf forest.

Everybody let Pedro just keep on thinking.

Other regular inhabitants of the valley included several families of striped skunks, almost as many ground squirrels as jackrabbits, a fox family, assorted gopher and king snakes, one great horned owl called Judge Wendell, and several dozen fence swift lizards.

Occasional visitors to the valley were the few mule deer who came down when snow pushed them from the higher peaks of the Coast Range, a few coyotes, and Trap, the great golden eagle who glided on his broad wings over a range seven times as large as the little valley.

For color and beauty, there were the flowers that came after the winter rains had once more filled little Santa Ysabel Creek, in the bottom of the valley.

There were burr clover and filarec, red maids, phacelia, and huge bursts of California golden poppies.

All the plants and animals formed an ancient community that had been worked out in the time of Finsterhall's ancestors, perhaps a thousand grandfathers ago.

Every living thing there knew who should eat what (or, on occasion, whom), who could grow in another's shade, and what contribution each should make to keep the community in balance.

But, it was a delicate balance. And what would happen to it if an elephant suddenly did step on the scales?

Finsterhall shuddered at the thought, then

shook it off and went looking for some tender green shoots for dinner.

Elephants indeed! If he kept thinking like that, the next thing he might imagine he saw would be something really weird like a giraffe.

The next thing Finsterhall saw was a giraffe.

He fainted dead away.

It was dark when Finsterhall came to on the little rise about a hundred hops from his burrow. His eyes quickly darted from side to side, looking for movement in the moonless night. And his nose sniffed the night air for danger.

That was a crazy thing to do, he thought to himself. Even a bobcat as dumb as Pedro could catch an unconscious rabbit, if the rabbit was out in the open.

And whoever heard of a rabbit fainting? Well, nobody was going to hear about it from Finsterhall. He would be the joke of the valley.

But it had been such a crazy day. First, there had been that track. At least, it certainly looked like a track. Then that business of seeing what looked for all the world like a giraffe, nibbling on the top leaves of one of the scrub oaks about a half mile away, near the foot of Fox Peak.

Was Finsterhall's mind playing jokes on him? Had he imagined the giraffe? But that was ridiculous. Why would he suddenly imagine a gi-

Elephants indeed! The next thing he might imagine he saw would be something really weird — like a giraffe.

The next thing Finsterhall saw was a giraffe.

He fainted dead away.

raffe? And Joe had seen the track, too, even if he wouldn't admit it was a track.

Finsterhall strained his eyes in the direction of Fox Peak, but it was much too dark now to even see the outline of the little hill where the red fox family lived.

"Boy, talk about weird," he said to himself. And he began making his way homeward in the blackness. Just before he reached the burrow hole, he bumped into Joe.

"Yipes!" said Joe. "Hey, wow, Finst, you nearly gave me a heart attack. Don't come creeping up on a guy like that in the dark."

"Sorry," said Finst. "I guess I didn't realize I was hopping so quietly. My nerves are a little edgy tonight."

"Don't tell me you've found some more elephant tracks."

"No. Not exactly. But there's something awfully strange going on in this valley, and I need some answers. If you'll go with me, I'd like to go talk to Judge Wendell. He knows more about what's happening in this valley than anyone, except maybe Trap."

"I don't know, Finst," said Joe. "I mean, I'd like to go with you, but, well … uh …"

"But you're afraid of the dark."

"Who says I'm afraid of the dark?" said Joe, puffing up his chest just a bit. "I'm not afraid of any old dark night."

"Fine. Let's go."

"Wait a minute! It's just that I'm ... I'm ... well, I'm just not all that curious about an old hole in the ground."

"Now, listen, Joe. You're going to be darn curious if there really is an elephant somewhere around here and he happens to step on your hole in the ground."

Joe shrugged his shoulders. "Oh, okay, I'll go with you. But I'll bet the Judge laughs at you when you tell him you've been seeing elephant tracks."

"Well, if he laughs at that," said Finsterhall, "I've got something else that will put him in hysterics."

"What's that?" asked Joe, starting that nervous twitch in his nose again.

"Come on," said Finsterhall. "I'll tell you when we get there."

II

Clumsy Bobcat on the Prowl

It was a perfect night for hunting, and Pedro had the smell of bird in his nose. He had picked up the scent some fifteen minutes before, and had begun his stalk.

At first, the scent was very weak and would drift in and out with every little change in the evening breeze. But now it was strong and steady, and growing stronger all the time.

Pedro padded quietly down the hillside, carefully picking each step and avoiding crackling leaves and twigs.

The only noise to be heard was the growling of his stomach.

It had been three days since Pedro had eaten, and that hadn't been much of a meal. Some picnickers down by the creek had left a part of a pastrami sandwich and some potato chips.

Pedro couldn't remember a day when his

stomach hadn't growled. It growled because he was hungry most of the time, and he was hungry most of the time because his stomach growled and scared away anything he was trying to sneak up on.

It was an embarrassing vicious circle.

Pedro just didn't seem to have the knack of being a bobcat down right. Something seemed to be missing.

Like that time he fell out of the scrub oak. Any other cat would have landed on his feet. Pedro landed on his head.

(Actually, any other cat probably wouldn't have fallen out of a tree in the first place.)

But tonight, the scent was there, and it stayed there. It didn't flit off into the wind like bird scents usually did. It kept coming in steadily from wherever it was, some distance on down in the valley. Perhaps, Pedro thought, it was a bird that couldn't fly away for some reason. He kept trying to imagine how a real meal, caught all by himself, would really taste.

But it was hard to imagine. He had nothing to compare it with.

Still, the scent came on. And now there was a sliver of moonlight. Not enough to hinder Pedro's stalk, but just enough to give him a helpful trace of light.

He picked a path that would take him through a thick growth of sage and other small brush,

Pedro, the clumsy bobcat, made a perfect stalk following the scent of the bird in the night. But he hadn't quite expected to find this much bird.

"G-g-good evening," he said. "W-w-welcome to San Pasqual ... uh ... SIR!"

19

perfect cover for him in case his prey suddenly was alerted.

Slowly, softly he crept, and the excitement was growing in his heart. He could feel his pulse drumming in his neck, and even the stomach growling seemed to have quieted a bit as a successful hunt seemed nearer and nearer.

Pedro stopped near a big yucca plant, the one called "Candle of the Lord," to pin down the exact source of the scent and to plan his final few steps.

He was out of the stretch of brush now, and the scent was coming from just a short distance away. The faint moonlight was bright enough to see for some distance ahead, and the ground was clear — except for one big manzanita tree about thirty yards ahead and to the right. The bird had to be just on the other side of it.

Trying to wind his way through the manzanita would be too risky. Pedro knew the tree, and it was silver with age and nearly dead. It was also thick and tangled, and there were too many tiny branches and needles which could be accidentally brushed against and broken off in the dark.

A noise like that would frighten the bird away, if it could fly. Pedro decided to use the manzanita as a blind, creep up on it, then simply walk around it and pounce on the bird.

The final stalk was on.

He crept so slowly it took him nearly ten minutes to cover the thirty yards. Tensing his muscles for the final spring, he began working his way around the tree.

In the final seconds, his anticipation stripped away all caution and, in a sudden burst, he streaked around to the other side of the tree and came face to face with his prey. Or, rather, face to ankle.

Standing there in the moonlight was his bird. And, sure enough, it was completely helpless to fly.

It was an eight-foot tall, three hundred pound ostrich!

Pedro gulped a double swallow of night air, looked up into the moon glint of the giant bird's eyes, and stammered out: "G-g-good evening. W-w-welcome to S-San Pasqual ... uh ... SIR!"

Then he whirled on his paws and streaked off in the dark as if he had been shot out of a cannon.

And his stomach growl grew fainter and fainter until it disappeared in the night.

III

A Visit to the Judge

Judge Wendell's tree was about a fifteen minute hop from the burrows of Finsterhall and Joe, if the hop was made in daylight. However, it took more than twice that long for the rabbit cousins as they groped along the valley, first in total darkness, then by the faint light of a tiny slice of moon.

When they reached the tree, Finsterhall whispered: "Psst, Judge Wendell. It's Finsterhall and Joe."

The great horned owl said: "Who?"

"Finsterhall and Joe, the rabbit cousins from the burrows south of here."

Judge Wendell stared down at his two visitors, blinked his huge shining eyes, and said: "Surely you don't expect me to remember the names of every single rabbit in San Pasqual. Why, there must be thousands of you. In any case, what can I do for you?"

"Well," said Finsterhall, raising his voice a little higher than a whisper, "I've seen some strange things today, and I thought perhaps you might be able to tell me something about them."

"What sort of strange things, my young friend?"

"First of all, I found a huge track of something. It must have been at least a foot across."

"All tracks are exactly one foot across," said the Judge. "Unless, of course, they are tire tracks. Then they are one tire across."

"I never thought of that," said Joe.

"When I say a foot across," said Finsterhall, "I mean it was twelve inches across. And it looked suspiciously like an elephant track, with stubby toes and everything."

"I see," said the old owl, with a voice that seemed to have suddenly grown grave. "You said a minute before that you had seen some strange 'things.' What other strange things did you see."

"Well," said Finsterhall, haltingly, "I can't be sure, but I think ... I'm almost sure ... I saw a ... a giraffe."

"You what?" said Joe. "Aw c'mon, Finst!"

"Quiet, young rabbit," said the judge. "Now then, Fosterwall ..."

"It's Finsterhall, sir."

Finsterhall explained the strange sights he had seen to the wise old owl, Judge Wendell. The judge had seen even more and promised a thorough inspection of the valley and the new strangers who had moved into it.

"Very well, Finsterhall. Where exactly did you see this giraffe, and which way did he go?"

"I think I saw him, that is, whatever I saw, I saw near the foot of Fox Peak. And I don't know where he went, because the next thing I knew it was dark."

"You mean it suddenly flipped from light to dark in a twinkling?" asked the judge.

"Not exactly, your honor. I ... I sorta went to sleep in kind of a hurry."

"You what?"

"I fainted."

At this, Joe began laughing hysterically. He rolled over on his back and was holding his sides, as tears of laughter streamed down his furry face.

The judge's voice boomed: "Young rabbit, when you get through having whatever kind of fit you are having, perhaps you will be kind enough to afford myself and Funstermall here ..."

"It's Finsterhall, sir."

"Yes, hrummp. As I said, perhaps you can afford us a few brief moments of silence so that we can continue our conversation about this giraffe your cousin saw."

"But, your honor," said Joe, controlling his giggles enough to talk, "surely you don't think there is some slight chance that Finst really did see a giraffe?"

"No, I don't think there is some slight chance," said the judge. "I think there is a very good chance. Because, I happened to see three of them myself today."

"But, what's happening, sir?" pleaded Finsterhall. "What in the world is happening? We've never had giraffes in this valley. And, do you think there really is an elephant?"

Joe just stood there stunned. He was no longer laughing, although his mouth was hanging wide open. And his nose was twitching about as fast as he could twitch it.

"I don't know — yet," said the judge, solemnly. "That is, I know a few answers, but not all of them. I hope to know the rest in a few days. The giraffes are here, that much is certain. As for an elephant, I have not seen one. However, I have been away a few days and returned only late this afternoon. But I saw some other things besides the giraffes as I flew in over the south end of the valley."

"W-w-what, sir?" Joe managed to ask, although he was almost afraid of getting an answer.

"I saw a small herd of zebras, the horse with black and white stripes. They were eating hay out of a trough somebody had placed under an oak. And, I saw what appears to be a metal fence around the end of the valley. There was no fence there before."

"What do you think we should do, judge?" asked Finsterhall.

"I think you should go home and go to bed and wait until I make a complete inspection of the valley early tomorrow morning. Then, perhaps, I can give a full report to you and the others who live in the valley. You and your friends and relatives may return here at twilight tomorrow, and I will tell you what I know. In the meantime, remember that neither you nor I have seen anything that would intentionally hurt you. A giraffe, a zebra, indeed, even an elephant would have very little interest in a rabbit."

"You mean we're safe from them?" asked Finsterhall.

"I see no reason why you should not be," said the judge, "as long as you do not stand in their footprints at the same time they are standing in them."

"Y-yes, sir. Then, we'll be getting on home, and see you tomorrow. Goodnight, your honor."

"Goodnight, Hasterfall."

"It's Finsterhall, sir."

"Hmmmp, yes, indeed, Finsterhall. And goodnight to you too, James."

Joe did not even bother to correct the old owl. He was sticking too close to Finsterhall, as they felt their way back home through the darkness.

IV

'But Beware the Cheetah'

The story of the strange animals spread rapidly throughout the valley the next day. It passed underground, through the network of rabbit and squirrel burrows and lizard nests. By mid-afternoon, almost every native resident of the valley had some information on the newcomers.

In fact, a lot of them had some information that really didn't even exist.

Everytime the story was related through another twist in the underground hallways, it got another twist to it.

One version had it that a circus train had derailed nearby, and the valley was filled with escaped animals and clowns.

Another claimed that Africa had been all built up with suburbs, and the animals were all swimming across the ocean to San Pasqual.

Even the little colony of red ants that lived in its sunbaked anthill on the valley floor had a version. It wasn't elephants that had come to San Pasqual. It was anteaters!

The gossip about the new neighbors hummed under the valley, and whenever anybody ran out of facts, they just made some new ones up.

Now and then, one of the animals would poke his head out, take a quick look around, and pop back into the safety of the ground. But no one ventured out of a burrow that day, until twilight neared.

Then they began making their way cautiously to the tree of old Judge Wendell.

They moved on the valley by the hundreds. Squirrels darting from bush to bush, popping down into a stranger's burrow every few feet, then popping back up and continuing on. The rabbits ran from sage to rocks to tall grass, stopping now and then in the shade and trying to listen for sounds above the noise of their own heartbeats.

The lizards were little more than gray blurs as they streaked full speed toward the judge's tree.

The judge was waiting for them.

He stood patiently on his favorite limb and waited for the chattering to cease. Finally, when they saw he would not speak until it did, the din suddenly became silence.

"Now then," said the judge, "perhaps we can bring this meeting to order."

Four dozen different animals suddenly asked four dozen different questions all at once.

"Quiet!" said the judge. Silence again.

"My friends," said the judge, after clearing his throat, "I have spent a good part of the day flying over and inspecting San Pasqual Valley. Furthermore, I have also spent some time listening to a group of men who are working at the far western end of the valley."

"Men?" said one of the squirrels. "There aren't any men in that section of the valley."

"There are men," said the judge, and the squirrel grew silent.

"There are men — and there are animals. They are here, indeed."

"An elephant?" asked Finsterhall. "Did you see an elephant, judge?"

"Fastertall, I ..."

"It's Finsterhall, sir."

"Finsterhall, I saw twelve elephants today, both of the African and the Asian variety. And it is my understanding that there will be more."

The crowd of little animals gasped.

"Not only are there elephants, but we now live among the giant rhinoceros — several of

Twelve elephants were among the first arrivals at the Wild Animal Park. Also moving into the peaceful little valley were lions, zebras, deer, tortoises, gorillas and — men.

them — and zebras, huge tortoises, many different kinds of antelope, assorted deer, lions ..."

"L-lions?" stammered Joe.

"Lions," said the judge. "Not to mention the cape buffalo, giraffes, a two-ton Indian gaur, which is the largest of all wild cattle, and ..."

"Please, sir," interrupted Finsterhall, "what are they DOING here?"

"Yes, Fost ... ahem ... my young friend, I was just coming to that. What are they doing here? Well, according to the conversation I overheard from the men, this is their new home. They are living here."

"But ..."

"Patience, patience. Let me explain a little more. Now, some thirty miles from here, in the city, is the San Diego Zoo, one of the world's largest and most famous zoos. Yes, well, now it seems that the men who run this zoo decided sometime ago to open sort of a branch operation out here. Not exactly a zoo, but a place where animals could roam in much more freedom and perhaps live happier, healthier lives."

"Healthier for who?" asked Finsterhall. "The idea of lions in my neighborhood doesn't make me feel particularly healthy."

"Yeah," said Joe. "A lamebrained bobcat is one thing, but a bunch of full-sized lions — well, I think it's time for me to start planning a long trip."

"I think that is something you might regret," said the judge, "for the men are not only bringing these new animals here, but they are also bringing food. Lots of food. More than enough for the animals, and more than enough for us. I should think all of our diets will improve considerably in a short time. Also, the men are bringing in water — plenty of water. And you know how little water there is around here during the summer months."

"Yes," said Finsterhall, "but lions eat rabbits!"

Finsterhall knew this, not from personal knowledge, but from the bank of animal information he was born with. It had been acquired over tens of thousands of years, and passed down from generation to generation.

It is that way with all animals. The young eagle, kicked out of his nest by his father without instruction, still knows what he can and cannot eat, and that he must someday fly and hunt.

In the same way, Finsterhall had recognized the giraffe when he saw him, even though he had never seen a giraffe before. Some ancestor, perhaps ages ago, had seen one.

And, in a like manner, everything Finsterhall learned during his lifetime would be passed on to his children.

"True," said the judge. "Lions do eat rabbits.

That is the scheme of things in the wilds. But, even there, the rabbit is something of a last resort of a hungry lion, and is pursued only when he cannot find bigger game.

"However, this is not to be wild land, anymore. San Pasqual is to be — in fact, it already is — the new San Diego Wild Animal Park. And every animal within its borders will be fed a balanced diet.

"As for the lions, I think you will find them rather lazy creatures who haven't the slightest inclination to bother themselves about some skinny little rabbit when they are being given their fill of steak each day by the men."

Just the same, Finsterhall thought to himself, he'd hate to have one of those fainting spells in front of a lion. He might faint near one that wasn't as lazy as the others.

The judge continued talking: "You will find that the animals already here, and those still to come, have enclosures which, though quite large enough for them to roam around in, confine them to a certain area. There are fences, and there are huge, concrete ditches to keep them in their own areas.

"Some of the animals will be mixed in with others. For instance, the ostrich gets along quite well with the zebra and the rhinoceros and the antelope. The lions will be by themselves, unless some of you want to go visit them.

"Most of the animals are vegetarians, so the only worry you might have from them is getting underfoot."

"I wouldn't especially care to have an elephant sit on me, either," Joe whispered to Finsterhall.

"Shhhhh!" said Finsterhall, "just watch out for a lot of sudden shade."

"I should warn you all," said the judge, "there is one animal that could be extremely dangerous if you are not careful."

"What's that?" asked several in the crowd.

"The cheetah," said the judge. "The cheetah will not be on public display at first, as the rest of the animals will, but he will be kept in a long cage-like enclosure known as the cheetah run, and will be studied by the men.

"The cheetah is not lazy. If you somehow happened to stumble into his cage, he would come after you even if he had eaten a dozen steaks. However, it would be hard for you to accidentally get into his cage, since the bottom of it is covered with chicken-wire which goes quite a ways underground, to prevent him from digging out. Still, my advice is to stay away."

"Thanks a lot, judge," said Joe, not quite loud enough for anybody to hear. "That's advice I had already given myself."

With this, the meeting broke up and Finsterhall and Joe, with the others, made their way
homeward in the dusk.

V

Sherman, Who Looks Like a Tank

"But I want to see one!" said Finsterhall, as his eyes darted around the morning landscape from the entrance of his burrow. "The judge said we haven't anything to fear, and I want to see one."

Joe was trying to hold him back.

"For Pete's sake, Finst, can't you just leave well enough alone? Suppose you do see a rhinoceros, but suppose he doesn't see you? Do you know how much those things weigh? They go up to five tons. Why, if he accidentally stepped on you, there wouldn't be enough of you left for a teacup of rabbit stew."

But Finsterhall's mind was made up. "I'll go by myself if you don't want to come, Joe, but I'm going. And I'm going this morning, in the daylight, so I can see what I'm looking at."

Joe shrugged, twitched his nose, and fell in

behind his headstrong cousin. "Ridiculous," he muttered to himself. "A whole four pounds of rabbit going out to meet ten thousand pounds of rhino."

"Did you say something?" asked Finsterhall.

"Nothing," said Joe. "Nothing at all."

The entire valley was splashed with morning sunshine as the two little rabbits made their way cautiously toward the southeast end of the park, where the judge said he had seen the herd of giant white rhinos.

They stopped once for a short breakfast of sweet clover, and Joe popped down a California golden poppy for desert. They were one of his weaknesses.

The two rabbits kept glancing upward from time to time, checking the sky for danger. There would be nothing to fear from Pedro at this time of day. He would be curled up and sleeping somewhere in the shadows, and his growling stomach would serve as an alarm, anyway.

But somewhere, gliding high above the ground and watching sharply for movement below, was Trap, the golden eagle, the fiercest and fastest hunter in the hills.

It was said that when Trap made his dive on some hapless victim, he became like an invisible and silent arrow. And his claws were made of steel.

Trap never went hungry.

Some distance from their home, the two young rabbits went over a slight rise in the land and suddenly stopped. A few hundred yards away they saw a small pond of water that had not been there before.

"That's funny," said Finsterhall. "Do you suppose that is some of the water the men brought?"

"I don't know," said Joe. "Let's go down and get a drink, though. It should still be nice and cool at this time of day."

A few minutes later, Finsterhall and Joe were sipping a refreshing drink in the shade of a boulder at the edge of the little pool.

Suddenly, the boulder stood up.

"Eeeeeeyyyyykkk!" Joe yelled as the two rabbits streaked full speed into a patch of tall grass a few yards away.

They stood there panting and trembling as they watched the boulder take a casual drink of water.

"That's ... that's him," whispered Finsterhall.

"Who?"

"That's one of the white rhinos."

"He doesn't look white to me," said Joe.

"Dummy. White rhinos aren't really white.

Finsterhall and Joe went down to the pond for a cool drink of water. While they were sipping a refreshing drink in the shade of a boulder at the edge of the pool, the boulder suddenly stood up.

It was Sherman, the white rhino.

They're just a lot lighter than other rhinos. Golly, how much do you suppose he weighs?"

"About as much as you and I and all our relatives, past and present, put together," said Joe. "Let's get out of here."

"No. I want to talk to him."

"Are you out of your hopping mind, Finst? What in the world have you got to talk about with a rhinoceros? You couldn't possibly have anything in common."

"How do I know that until I find out?" said Finsterhall. "We were both thirsty, weren't we. That's something in common."

"Yeah," said Joe, "and Trap and Pedro both get thirsty now and then, but I don't see you setting up any round tables with them about it."

"That's different. Rhinos aren't meat eaters. They're vegetarians, like us. They probably even like golden poppies."

"I hope not," said Joe. "That baby looks like he could eat every golden poppy in this entire valley for lunch today, if he wanted to. C'mon, Finst, let's go."

"Nope. I'm going to talk to him." And the little rabbit began taking short, cautious hops from the patch of grass toward the great, gray creature at the edge of the pool.

Joe followed him, but not very closely.

"H-hello," said Finsterhall, nervously, as he

got to within a few yards of the rhino. The lumbering giant turned slowly around, squinted down at Finsterhall, and then at Joe behind him, and said, in a gentle and friendly voice, "Good morning. When did they bring you here?"

"Oh, we ... we've always been here," said Finsterhall. "Well, not always, but all our lives so far. We were born here. I'm Finsterhall and back there is my cousin Joe."

Joe smiled a toothy kind of smile that looked plain silly on the face of a rabbit.

"Well, I've only been here two days," said the rhino, "and it seems like a most amazing place. My name is Sherman."

Finsterhall, now warming up to the conversation, stepped in a little closer and said: "Welcome to San Pasqual Valley, Sherman. Did you come from Africa?"

"No," said Sherman, "I came from the San Diego Zoo. I suppose I was born there. At least, I've lived there as long as I can remember. It's a pretty nice place, and I had a large area to run in, but nothing like this. This ... this somehow seems more like home to me, and I've only been here two days. You say this place is called San Pasqual?"

"Yep," said Finsterhall. "San Pasqual Valley. Me and Joe know the whole valley. We could show you around if you wanted, or answer any questions you might have."

Flashing through Finsterhall's mind was the idea of what an advantage it might be to have a friend this big walking beside you. Why, a rabbit could walk right up to old Pedro, if he had a rhino pal by his side.

"Thanks," said Sherman, "but I've got more room right here than I know what to do with, yet. Tell me, what other animals are there around here?"

Joe now stepped in and joined the conversation.

"Oh, there are lots of us rabbits, and ground squirrels, and some snakes, and a stupid old bobcat. Some foxes, lizards and Judge Wendell, the owl. Those are all natives, of course. Then there's the new animals, like you, that they are bringing in. Elephants and lions and I don't know what all. Finst and I decided today we'd go out and meet a few of the newcomers and sorta welcome 'em, you know."

"That's very friendly of you," said Sherman. "I think I'm going to enjoy it here very much. Very much, indeed." .

"Well, we'd better get going, Sherman," said Finsterhall. "It's a pretty long way back to where we live. Anyway, welcome once again."

"Thank you. And stop by for a drink anytime."

The two cousins began moving away, but after only a few hops, the rhino called to them.

"By the way, are there any tanks here in the valley?"

Finsterhall stopped with a puzzled look on his face. "I don't think so," he said. "I don't really know. What's a tank anyway?"

"I don't know, but I always wanted to meet one. I guess they must be about my size, because half the people who passed my enclosure in San Diego would always say, 'He looks like a tank, doesn't he?'"

"If we see one, we'll let you know, Sherman," said Finsterhall. And the two rabbits headed for home.

VI
Nairobi Village Goes Up

New animals arrived almost every day now at San Pasqual, and Finsterhall and Joe made the trip to the western end of the park boundary at least twice a week to watch the men unload the newcomers, and to take a look at the progress of the strange buildings that were being erected.

The buildings were in a cluster around some big ponds of water, and the rabbits had heard the men refer to the area as Nairobi Village. But the buildings looked nothing like the plain, white farmhouses in the south end of the valley, outside the park boundary. They seemed to be built of poles and reeds, mud and grass.

"You'd think," said Joe, "if they are building a brand new park, they could afford to get some more modern materials."

And the rabbits heard the men talk about the park being nearly ready to open to the public.

"What's 'the public,' Finst?" asked Joe.

"Why, it's people," said Finsterhall. "Men and women, and children, who will come to the park to see all the animals. Remember how Sherman talked about the people coming to see him at the zoo? Well, that's what they'll do out here, too."

They watched the men complete a huge aviary at the main entrance to the park, and they were there the day some other men released hundreds of bright colored birds of all sizes inside it.

The rabbits sat in the shade of a pile of grass thatches and watched the last touches put on the park's animal hospital, a place where injured and infant animals could be cared for.

"I wonder if they'd mind checking out my back," said Joe. "I get these pains some days."

"That's for the park animals," said Finsterhall. "Not for us. They aren't putting all this stuff up just for plain old jackrabbits like us."

And they were there the day the gorillas arrived, and were placed in their enclosure on the western edge of the village. Once released into their area, the gorillas ran and rolled, did somersaults, splashed in their small pool, and hung upside down, rightside up, and every which way from their different climbers.

The gorillas looked fierce, but their antics soon had Finsterhall and Joe rolling on the ground in hysterical laughter. San Pasqual was getting to be a lot more fun than it was in the old days.

Then, they would suddenly stop, sit down, and make faces.

Finsterhall and Joe watched them for more than an hour, and never had a dry eye all that time. They were crying with laughter at those crazy clowns.

San Pasqual was getting to be a lot more fun than it was in the old days.

Of course, both rabbits had seen the elephants by now. There were two bands of them in two different enclosures. The Asian elephants with the big, rounded heads, and the African ones with the huge raggedy ears. One of the African elephants, the big female they called Hatari, had been in a movie when she was only a baby, they had heard. It didn't impress them, particularly, because neither Finsterhall nor Joe had the slightest idea what a movie might be.

Still, the elephants themselves did impress the rabbits. It was hard to believe anything that big could actually be alive and move. The sight of them simply took the cousins' breath away.

They especially liked to watch the Asian elephants in the late afternoon, when they would trot off single file to their water hole. There, the keeper would give them a shower with a hose, while the elephants kept tossing dust over their shoulders and onto their huge backs.

"Maybe it's what the elephants call a mud bath," suggested Finsterhall.

"It doesn't seem to be doing their complexion much good," replied Joe.

On their way back home from the village area, Finsterhall and Joe would stop off at some of the feeding troughs in the various areas, and fill themselves on leftovers. Judge Wendell had been right about the food. The rabbits were now adding to their regular diet such items as alfalfa pellets, chopped carrots, celery and various other raw vegetables.

Their coats were turning shiny and sleek with the extra food, and both of them were gaining weight. Finsterhall and Joe now weighed over five pounds — put together.

VII

Pedro Drops in on Relatives

"What do you want?" asked the lion.

"I want my mama," said Pedro.

That ignorant little bobcat had done it again. This time he'd got himself caught inside the lions' den.

Now it had never occurred to Pedro to try to stalk a woodpecker, but he was so hungry that afternoon that he would have stalked a rock if he had thought he could get any nourishment from it. Besides, he thought, he might actually have a chance to get that woodpecker. It was pecking its head off in a big scrub oak that stood right on the edge of a small arroyo.

And it was pecking so hard and making so much noise, it couldn't possibly hear Pedro's telltale stomach growl.

Pedro inched his way through the brush toward the oak. He froze and crouched low when the bird suddenly stopped pecking, but moved again when the bird resumed its rat-tat-tat-tat on the limb. A few minutes later, he was at the base of the tree.

Slowly he began climbing the tree. He stopped once, closed his eyes and clenched his teeth when his claws slipped and made a scratching noise which he thought sure would give him away. But, no, the bird didn't hear. He just kept pecking.

Easy, Pedro thought. Easy, easy, easy. Now he was actually on the same limb as the bird. Almost within springing distance. Just a little bit more. Just a little ...

Pedro sprang.

The bird went flying.

The rotted limb broke.

Pedro went flying.

Down.

The limb had been hanging far over the rim of the arroyo, and, in fact, even over the tall chain fence that ran along the edge of the little dry canyon. Pedro rode that rotten limb in something of a power dive, right into the fenced-in portion.

He crashed with a painful jar and found himself staring whisker to whisker with a pride of more than a dozen full grown lions.

Often when faced with a sudden emergency,

Pedro crashed with a jar into a pride of more than a dozen full grown lions. The ignorant little bobcat had goofed again.

some creatures will react with such surprise that they don't have time to be frightened.

In Pedro's case, however, the bobcat reacted with such sudden fright that he didn't have time to be surprised that there were lions in the valley.

"What are you?" said the lion who had first spoken to him. "Some kind of a midget lion that flies? If so, you aren't very good at it, are you?"

"No sir ... I mean, yes sir ... I mean, whatever you say, sir." Pedro's heart thumped like a bass drum, and his stomach roared like a tuba.

"Where's the rest of your tail?" said the lion. "And what's that noise? Are you growling at me?"

"Please, sir, you ... you ... I mean, we ... you and me, that is ... we must be some kind of distant relatives. You wouldn't eat a relative, would you?"

The other lions in the enclosure had paid little attention to Pedro. In fact, most of them actually appeared to be dozing in the afternoon sun. The others were quiet, except for an occasional swish of the tail aimed at a fly.

"A relative?" said the lion. "Well, I would hardly claim a tailless runt like you as a relative. On the other hand, I would hardly bother to eat you, either. In fact, you don't look like there's much there to eat other than a little scraggly fur and some bones. When's the last time you ate?"

Pedro's heart slowed down some upon receiving the good news that he would not be eaten, but his words still came in rather breathless gasps. Mostly from fear, but partly because he'd had just about every bit of wind knocked out of him in that fall.

"I ... I don't exactly remember, sir. I'm not ... not really very good as a hunter. At least, I've had a lot of bad luck lately."

Pedro did not mention that "lately" included that period of time from the day he was born to the present.

The old lion eyed him with a kind of grand boredom. Then he spoke again:

"Well, I suggest you trot yourself over to that west corner of our enclosure, where you'll find a couple of steaks left over from breakfast today. You might as well eat them before they go bad. After that, you'll find an opening along the south line of the fence which, if you squeeze hard enough, you should be able to get through. And I suggest you do just that, as soon as you're through with your meal."

Pedro was stunned. Steaks? For him? Real, honest to goodness, red meat steaks? Pedro, whose idea of a great meal was an abandoned hot dog, had never in his life suspected that he might someday sit down and dine on steak.

"Oh, thank you, sir, your highness ... I mean, your ... yes, thank you, thank you."

"Never mind all that," said the lion. "And you'd better drop by a couple of times a week to get a handout. While I certainly am not claiming you as a relative, you are a cat of sorts. I don't want something as scrawny as you running around this valley. I understand there are going to be tourists here, soon, and you could be bad for the whole cat image."

"Yes, sir, yes, sir. I'll certainly do that, sir," said Pedro, backing away from the great lion, in the direction of the steaks. "I surely will do that."

A few minutes later, Pedro was once again outside the fence. He had found the steaks, and he had dragged them through the small hole.

Now he sat in the shade of a squawbush and finished the first decent meal of his entire life. He was full and content, and overflowing with happiness because he would never again have to play that ridiculous game of trying to be a hunter. He could come back and eat steak with the lions.

Even his stomach had stopped growling.

Pedro had gone to heaven without even dying.

VIII

The Domain of the Eagle

At the northern rim of the valley, far above the ground, Trap glided silently on the warm currents drifting up from the oak covered hills. There was a glint of the late morning sun in his keen, yellow eyes as he watched every inch of the land below for movement. For prey.

The great golden eagle let the soft wind carry him in ever widening circles over San Pasqual. He was only slightly hungry, but he was infinitely patient. First he wanted to inspect all of the valley, which he had not seen for some three weeks. Then he would make his choice.

Trap had been hunting far to the north, seven valleys away. He used his huge range wisely and sparingly, a few days in one area, then on to another. Besides, there was no need to stay in one place. He was a lone eagle, the only one in the valleys, and had no use for a nest.

Trap, the golden eagle, glided silently on the warm currents drifting up from the oak covered hills. There was a glint of the late morning sun in his keen, yellow eyes. San Pasqual was one of the seven valleys he hunted.

As his circles finally carried him to the border of the park, he noticed the first of the changes. Then others, and still others. It was as if he had flown in over an entirely new valley, and yet it was the same.

He recognized the contours of the land. The hills and gullies remained the same. The big, broad valley was there, and the trees he knew.

But what were the odd, stick-like buildings below? And where in the world did so many huge and strange new creatures come from?

He saw the elephants and wondered at them. He circled twice over the curious gorillas, dipping dangerously lower than usual to make sure they were not some new kind of man.

He gazed at a large herd of gazelles browsing on a hillside, and he studied the beautiful impalas, with their graceful, lyre-shaped horns.

The ostriches, fifteen of them, caught his eyes and he knew they were birds. Not birds like him, with the freedom of the skies, but great, dignified members of his family, still.

Trap was not afraid of any of these animals. He had no fear of any living creature, except perhaps the man. None of the others could touch him. Only the man had an arm long enough to reach him, as he had learned the summer before when a man had pointed a smoky finger into the sky and tore the life from Trap's mate, the beautiful Herta.

Still, Trap was awed by all the new creatures of the valley. It staggered his mind. How could such strange animals, and so many of them, suddenly find their way into this valley? He had seen nothing like them in any of his other valleys.

Now there were fences and moats, great water holes, and all these newcomers in this once wild valley.

Trap's wings carried him to the top of his favorite peak in the area, a rising where he had always stayed before while hunting in the valley. It was west and outside of the fences, but was high enough for him to sit and look over most of the broad expanse of the park.

And to think about these things.

He had been perched there, staring across the valley, several minutes before he noticed the smell of fresh meat in the air. It was near. Very near. And it was not the scent of a live creature. It was the blood smell.

With his lumbering, side-gait stride, Trap walked around the manzanita he had been standing against. And there it was.

A small, flat wooden box contained several chunks of fresh meat, neatly cut. It had been placed there, at the spot where Trap always returned, with purpose.

Trap's presence in the valley was known.

He took a chunk of the meat in his beak, shook it, smelled it, and threw it down in his testing. It seemed to bear no taint. It seemed good.

Trap ate.

Later that day, when evening was less than two hours away, Trap took another high tour of the valley. From a thousand feet in the air, Trap watched the new animals of the valley march toward their water holes or feeding troughs. He watched the giraffes munch on food that had been hung in bundles high in the scrub oaks.

All of the animals were being cared for. Their needs were being provided.

When he returned to his perch, Trap found fresh new chunks of meat in the wooden box.

Trap also was being cared for.

Well, it was not enough. Trap was no creature to be caged and pampered, to be fed like an infant. The food provided only half his needs. There was another half of Trap which needed to fly and hunt.

However, he could take these offerings on seldom occasions without any loss of dignity, he decided. So Trap ate again.

Then he sat and watched the darkness arrive.

Trap would return here on other days to rest, and look, and wonder. But never again would he hunt in this valley.

IX

The Hundred Foot Monster

It was late afternoon when Finsterhall saw the monster.

The thing was twenty times as long as any elephant he had ever seen, and it was coming right for him.

Finsterhall had been snacking on some green shoots at the southern end of the valley, some distance from the area where he and Joe usually roamed. Curiosity had brought them there more than hunger. Each day there seemed to be something new to see in the changing valley.

Now Finsterhall was nearly full, and he had turned to look for Joe when he saw it.

It had obviously stalked him, for Finsterhall had heard nothing. And now it was silently charging him.

In the instant before he bolted in terror, Finsterhall stared at the awesome thing bearing down on him. Nothing in his brain registered. There was no identification for it. But, it was monstrous. Perhaps a hundred feet long. Perhaps more. It moved snake-like toward him, and raised not a single particle of dust.

Now Finsterhall was tearing full speed through the brush and grass, his heart stuck in his throat, and panic pounding at his brain. He cut this way and that, darting blindly through unfamiliar growth. He was not looking for a hiding place. He was looking for distance between him and that ... that thing.

In his terror, he forgot about Joe. And he forgot about caution.

A small, tunnel-like opening through a thick growth of manzanita was suddenly in front of him, and he darted through it like a shot.

Suddenly, his small body slammed headlong into something hard and cold. The little rabbit's reflexes took over, and he dug his hind legs around to spin off the barrier. But the barrier did not give footing for his left leg. Instead, his leg slipped through it and stuck. Finsterhall, in panic, gave a sudden tug, but the leg did not come free.

Instead, there was a slight snap. And Finsterhall, for the second time in his life, fainted. But this time, he did so in pain.

His left hind leg was broken, and he was

caught and stuck in the chain link fencing and the overlapping chicken wire of the cheetah run.

It was nearly dark when Finsterhall regained consciousness. He moved his body and winced with pain. The broken leg had already swollen, lodging it tighter in the wire. There was no chance now of pulling it free.

Finsterhall tried to listen above the sound of his heart. He knew where he was. He knew it the instant he saw the wire-lapped fencing. He remembered the words of Judge Wendell.

But he didn't know where the cheetah was.

The run was long. Several hundreds of feet. There was room for the cheetah to get out and really give himself a good run. The great steel-spring muscles of the fastest killer alive needed that kind of room to keep their edge.

Finsterhall took trembling stock of his situation.

He had come right through the manzanita tunnel, and with the setting sun in his eyes, had not even seen the fencing. He was outside the cheetah cage, but his leg was inside. Besides, the chicken wire only went up about a foot on the chain link. It wouldn't be much trouble for the cheetah to reach over it and scoop Finsterhall up in a razor clawed paw.

San Pasqual Valley, with its new wild animal park, did not seem like such a fun place anymore to the terrified little rabbit.

The hundred-foot-long monster with the blazing eye was silently charging Finsterhall. The little rabbit, his heart stuck in his throat and panic pounding at his brain, never realized he was running toward more danger — the cheetah enclosure.

Finsterhall didn't know whether he was caught at one end of the run or the other, or somewhere in the middle. The darkness, and brush growing along the edge of the run in both directions made it impossible to tell.

His mind returned to the monster that had made him run into this trap. But it did not linger there. Whatever it was that had chased him was an unknown factor, but the danger of the cheetah was very real. Sooner or later it would come along this section of the run. And when it did, it would see or smell Finsterhall.

The night closed in around Finsterhall.

With it came the noises of the darkness. Birds and crickets began their chanting choruses, and somewhere, far away in another valley, the lonesome moan of a coyote poured into the night.

Finsterhall lay very still. It was the only thing in the world he could do.

Two, then three hours passed. A chillness swept over the valley floor and into the rabbit's aching body. He clenched his teeth and tried hard not to shiver. The sound of chattering teeth might bring unwanted company.

Suddenly the night air split with a sound that practically hardened the blood in Finsterhall's two-and-a-half pound body. A piercing, high-pitched shriek. The cry of the cheetah.

He was somewhere in the run.

The cry seemed to come from some distance to the north. Being scared didn't stop Finsterhall's thinking. Then he was caught at the south end of the run. Perhaps not all the way down at the end, but pretty near it.

Was the cheetah's cry a signal that he was about to begin one of his streaking dashes down the run? If so, by the time he reached the end of it, he would catch the scent of live rabbit in the air. A live rabbit in a snare.

Silence. Nothing.

It was as if all the insects, lizards and night-birds had heard the cry and had stopped their skittering about and singing to wait and see what happened next.

More silence.

Then, in the distance, a muffled pounding of padded feet.

Fast. Very fast. And growing in volume.

Finsterhall could hear them because his ears were ten times sharper than they ever had been during his life. And because the night had grown so suddenly quiet.

The cheetah was coming.

X

Death Eyes of the Cheetah

The big cat with the small head, pointed ears, and bullets for feet, raced down the run and, in a matter of seconds, passed the spot where Finsterhall was snagged in a blur the little rabbit could not even see. The truth is, Finsterhall could not have seen the cheetah if it had been running in slow motion in broad daylight. His eyes were shut tight, and his body was positively paralyzed.

But the cheetah had passed him.

The graceful killer reached the end of the run, some twenty yards past Finsterhall in a fraction of a second. He came to a sudden stop, and sucked in a deep swallow of the cold air. A good run! His muscles quivered with life. And his eyes, yellow and cold as old coins, drilled two holes in the night.

Now, run again!

Once again he shot down the run, as if he had been loosed from a bowstring.

Once again he sped past Finsterhall, and his padded pounding faded away to the north.

Why? Finsterhall asked himself this as his hurting lungs stopped holding and took in a breath. What had happened? Why hadn't the giant cat caught a trace of Finsterhall in his nostrils? Why was Finsterhall of San Pasqual still alive?

The answer hit him right in the face, as soft as the night breeze.

The wind was blowing against him. He was downwind. The scent was carried away from the run. And it was night. The cheetah could not see him, crouched hurting in the darkness.

But the night winds change. And the darkness only lasts until morning.

The escape was narrow. But it could also only be counted as temporary. The wind might curl and change, and the cheetah might run again. And daylight was on its way.

Another hour passed, but it seemed more like an age, as Finsterhall lay listening and waiting. His broken leg was throbbing now, and the pain was great. Finally, when it reached a level more than he could bear, it blacked him out and he drifted off into a fitful sleep.

He dreamed of a cheetah the size of that big unknown monster, chasing him throughout the length of the valley, ever drawing closer and closer.

When he awoke, it was daybreak. The first fingers of the sun were reaching over the eastern hills and erasing the valley's night shadows.

Finsterhall did not look around to appraise his situation. He couldn't. His gaze was locked into one place.

He was staring into the pale, piercing eyes of the cheetah.

The big cat was about twelve feet away, the width of the run, directly across from Finsterhall. It was crouched and tense, its muscles coiled and ready to spring at any instant.

Finsterhall could do nothing but look. He could not even look away. And all of his other senses had left him. He could feel no pain anymore, and no morning chill. He could hear no noises of the valley. He could smell nothing.

He could only stare, spellbound, at the cold death in the cheetah's eyes.

Suddenly, Finsterhall's small body was being lifted up the side of the cage. But not by the claws of the cheetah. The big cat was still crouched in its place, and staring. Finsterhall was being lifted gently, and his leg was released from the wire carefully, by the hands of man. He quivered with new fear.

"Easy, there, little guy," the man said softly. "I'm not going to hurt you. You've got a lot less to worry about from me than from old Lonesome over there. What were you doing here, anyway? Volunteering for breakfast?"

The man carried Finsterhall over to a small truck parked a short distance away, and placed him in a little wire cage in the front seat.

"Now, relax, fella," he said. "The doctor is going to recommend a short stay for you in the village hospital. But you'll be out and good as new in no time."

A few minutes later, they pulled up to one of the buildings in the park village. And as the man lifted the cage from the car, Finsterhall saw the big monster that had chased him the night before.

But it was no monster at all. It was some kind of big vehicle with seats in it, and it was parked alongside a platform near the hospital on a single big metal rail. On its side were letters which spelled out "WGASA BUSH LINE."

It was simply a train of some kind to carry people around the five mile edge of the park.

At the hospital, the doctors set Finsterhall's leg and put a cast on it. They gave him some kind of liquid medicine that eased the pain, and they gave him a big bowl containing lettuce, carrot chunks, and alfalfa pellets. Then they set another bowl beside him with cool, clear water.

Finsterhall spent three weeks in his little cubicle in the hospital. They removed the cast after the second week, and he found he was able to move around on his injured leg if he did so rather gingerly. During the third week the strength returned to his leg.

Finally came the day when the man who had rescued Finsterhall picked him up and once more put him in the little cage in the truck. Then he started driving.

After several minutes, the man stopped the truck.

"Well, this looks like rabbit territory around here," he said. "I reckon it's as good as any place to set you loose." And the man lifted Finsterhall out of the cage and set him carefully on the ground.

"Now, don't go banging into old Lonesome's run anymore, you hear?" he yelled, as the little rabbit scooted away.

Finsterhall stopped about twenty yards away, and stood there getting his bearings. Yes, he knew exactly where he was. Home was still a good distance away, but he knew how to get there.

And so he headed off to find his burrow and, perhaps more important, to find Joe.

He had to talk to somebody.

Epilogue

Much of this little story you have just read is true.

They really do feed the golden eagle at San Diego Wild Animal Park in San Pasqual Valley, and he no longer hunts there.

A little bobcat really did stalk a bird scent until he came face to face with a giant ostrich.

Other animals, which could not live at peace in the park, such as coyotes and rattlesnakes, were captured and sent to zoos around the world in exchange for other stock. Being a dangerous rattlesnake in San Pasqual Valley did not mean destruction. In fact, it could mean a trip to Paris, or London, and free board and room the rest of your life. The staffs of the San Diego Zoo and Wild Animal Park are dedicated to the safety and preservation of all animal life, and a native jackrabbit of the valley is just as much a concern to them as some of the more exotic, imported animals.

And one more fact. If you are a rabbit in San Pasqual Valley, it definitely is not a good idea to go banging into the cheetah cage.

About the author

John Sinor is a syndicated newspaper columnist, author, university lecturer, screen writer, actor, husband and father.

Before becoming these things, he was a paper boy, flower seed salesman, high school halfback, carnival barker, and aspiring marine biologist.

He and his wife Diane, a drama teacher and actress, live in San Diego, Calif.

About the artist

Bud Root is a former newspaper illustrator who decided a few years ago to chuck all the stress of life in a metropolitan city and move with his wife to a place called Rainbow Valley in Indian, Alaska. There he planned to build his own house and work as a free lance artist.

He has done those things, and now reports he is busier than he has ever been in his life.